Charlotte

IN NATALIE'S

CW00741471

"William Mayne has produced some of the most surprising and exciting writing for children and his new story book could be tackled by a newly-confident reader or read aloud to younger ones... Natalie sees things happening and wants to do them, too, gets messy, whistles with her mouth full of milk – just an ordinary child, in fact, captured with enticingly feisty matter-of-factness." *Julie Myerson, The Mail on Sunday*

William Mayne has been one of this country's leading writers for young people for over forty years. In 1957 he was awarded the Carnegie Medal for *A Grass Rope* and since then has written stories on all manner of subjects – from the antics of a friendly household spirit in *The Hob Stories* to the extraordinary adventure *Antar and the Eagles*, which was shortlisted for both the Smarties Book Prize and the Whitbread Children's Novel Award. Among his other titles are *Earthfasts*, *Cradlefasts* and *Low Tide*, which won the 1993 Guardian Children's Fiction Award. He lives in some converted barns in the Yorkshire Dales.

For Natalie Harker
W.M.

In Natalie's Garden

Written by
WILLIAM MAYNE

Illustrated by
PENNY DALE

WALKER BOOKS
AND SUBSIDIARIES
LONDON • BOSTON • SYDNEY

First published 1998 by Walker Books Ltd
87 Vauxhall Walk, London SE11 5HJ

This edition published 1999

2 4 6 8 10 9 7 5 3 1

Text © 1998 William Mayne
Illustrations ©1998 Penny Dale

This book has been typeset in Plantin Light.

Printed in Great Britain by Clays Ltd, St Ives plc

British Library Cataloguing in Publication Data
A catalogue record for this book
is available from the British Library.

ISBN 0-7445-6393-3

CONTENTS

Next-door had floors on stalks outside, not inside,
because the men were still building it.

THE NEW HOUSE

Natalie wanted to wheel her wheelbarrow about inside the house and tip stuff out of it, *sploosh*, like the men next door. Wheel, wheel, wheel, they would go, and shout, and the *sploosh* would rush out of the front of the barrow for them to play with. They had big flat spoons called trowels for that.

The men had black wheelbarrows. Natalie's was yellow, like the wild dandelions in her new garden. She was bringing it up the back door steps. Dolls kept falling out of it. When they did, Natalie said "Sploosh," and picked them up again.

"No, Natalie," said Mum, coming to see

what was banging the door at the top of the steps. She was stirring something in a red bucket. "Play wheelbarrows in the garden. You'll bring in the mud."

Mum was wrong. The yellow barrow was full of dolls, not mud. "That's not how you play with wheelbarrows," said Natalie. "The men next door know how."

"They're builders," said Mum. "Of course they do."

"But so do I," said Natalie. "Sploosh." Another doll had jumped out.

"I'll call you in at tea-time," said Mum, still stirring the red bucket. "I'm busy in the house. It's so new it's never been decorated before."

"Let me see in the bucket," said Natalie, thinking something for tea was in it.

Mum showed her. It was like jelly, but not for tea.

"We won't like that," said Natalie, sniffing it. It smelt like carpet.

"It's wallpaper paste for the front room," said Mum. "If I do that, you wheelbarrow in the garden."

"I don't want to wheelbarrow in the garden," said Natalie. "I don't want to wheelbarrow in the front room even. I want to wheelbarrow upstairs. That's how the men do it next door."

"Natalie," said Mum, "you are not going to wheelbarrow in the house, not downstairs –"

"No," said Natalie.

"– or upstairs," said Mum.

"I don't want to wheelbarrow *inside* the house upstairs," said Natalie.

"I was just telling you that," said Mum. She went on stirring her red bucket. "No problem, then."

But Natalie meant something else. "I want to wheelbarrow upstairs but *outside* the house," she explained. "Like the men next door."

Some people might not understand, but Mum looked at the house next door, and knew what Natalie meant.

She saw the black wheelbarrow being wheeled about upstairs by the whistling boy, and outside as well. That house had floors on stalks *outside*, not inside, and the men were still building it.

The whistling boy waved to Mum, and she waved the pail back at him. Natalie waved too. Her yellow barrow tipped over, and dolls fell down the steps, *flop, flop, flop*, and *sploosh*. The black wheelbarrow next door tipped up too, and *sploosh* slid out onto the upstairs floor, the upstairs floor that was outside the house.

"That's what I want to do," said Natalie. "Upstairs and outside."

"I know what you mean," said Mum. "But we haven't any floors that are upstairs and outside."

"We'll go and look," said Natalie. "Me in the wheelbarrow and you pushing."

Mum put the red bucket on the top step, and Natalie into the yellow barrow. "We'll go right round our house," she said, "and have a look. Hold tight, barrowload."

Natalie held tight. She was her baby sister in a pram and fell asleep. She had seen babies do that. She closed her eyes. Her thumb tasted of mud.

"You look too," said Mum. "I won't see on my own."

They went down the path on one side, across the gravel where Daddy put the car, past the front lawn, which was turning green where Daddy had powdered it with seeds, then over a lumpy piece of garden. The wheelbarrow went *bump, bump, bump,* over the lumps. Dolls would fall out but Natalie held tight.

"Are you looking?" Mum asked.

"Yub," said Natalie, in a bumpy and floppy way.

"Can you see outside upstairs floors?" asked Mum.

"Nub," said Natalie, with her tongue falling out.

Beside Natalie's house there were no tall sticks to hold up an outside floor. Only the house next door had outside upstairs floors with wheelbarrows on them.

"Then that's it," said Mum, tipping Natalie out by the back door. "You wheelbarrow out here in the mud, while I put up some wallpaper, until tea-time."

"Then that's it," said Mum,
tipping Natalie out by the back door.

"Sploosh," said Natalie, falling out on the steps in a sort of thrown away heap like a baby.

The red bucket full of wallpaper paste rolled off the top step, and turned on its side. It filled Natalie's lap with paste, cold and sticky and smelling of carpet. It stuck her knees together.

"Natalie," said Mum.

"Mum!" said Natalie.

Mum did not hear, because the bucket fell over upside down on Natalie's head, like a huge hat right down to her shoulders.

Cold paste ran down her shirt and glued her arms to her side.

It walked into her nose, climbed in her ears, stuck in her eyes, and crawled into her mouth. It filled her hair and fixed her fingers together.

She stood up, and the bucket fell off, but

her feet slipped, and she sat down in sticky stuff.

"Sploosh," she said, and one side of her nose blew a bubble. It should have been fun, but her chin felt wobbly, and she thought it was going to cry. One of her eyes had a tear, all on its own.

"It only needed stirring," said Mum. "You didn't need to go swimming in it." She was not cross.

"Don't laugh," said Natalie, loudly.

"I wouldn't dream of it," said Mum.

"I meant the men," said Natalie.

The men next door with the barrow were laughing. They pretended to empty big black buckets over each other.

Only the whistling boy looked sorry for her.

"They think it's funny, that's all," said Mum.

"I don't," said Natalie. She had decided that.

"Nor do I," said Mum. "Get in the bucket and I'll carry you upstairs and tip you into the bath."

The bucket was too small for Natalie, but in the bath the sticky stuff melted away before she had time to laugh, or cry, or be cross. Mum washed her with new water until her hair was squeaky.

Daddy came home, wondering why there was no wallpaper and no tea. He dried Natalie, put her sleeping suit on her, and rubbed her hair fuzzy while she walked about on him.

"Somebody ate up all the paste," said Mum. "But I'll get tea for everyone else."

Natalie was ready to go out again to show Daddy that some houses have a floor upstairs and outside.

"After tea we'll look," said Daddy. "When all the men have gone home. They don't live here."

"They've got a wheelbarrow," said Natalie. "Same as me, and I live here."

When they went out to look there was no upstairs inside the house next door, except for thin bits of wood you could fall through. But round it, outside, there was a floor on stalks. "See," said Natalie.

"It's for wheelbarrows," said Daddy. "It's called scaffolding when it's outside."

Natalie nodded her head, because she knew all that.

Daddy put her to bed and read her a story until she was dreaming about red and black buckets.

The door handle was too high and heavy for Natalie when her arms were full of dolls.

DOLLS, TOYS, AND RABBITS

One rainy day a lady came to visit. Or perhaps it wasn't a person at all. She brought her black talking stick. Natalie knew about talking sticks because Grandpa had one. He would prod it into the ground with one hand, put the other hand to his ear, and say, "I can't hear you," when he really could.

Natalie was never sure about the lady, because of what happened when she left. When she came she put her black stick in the kitchen sink. Grandpa would never do that. She talked to Mum about shopping, and Mum talked to her, and they sat and had coffee.

Natalie had milk and looked out of the glass door at the wet garden and the yellow wheelbarrow. The wheelbarrow was full of water. The top of the water was full of splash-marks, and water was dripping from the wheelbarrow's chin.

All the dolls and toys wanted to have a swimming ride straight away. But the door handle was too high and heavy for Natalie when her arms were full of dolls. Dolls and toys got too excited and fell down.

The lady with the talking stick finished her coffee and got the stick from the sink. She nearly trod on Natalie and almost had her toe on a toy.

"Oh, look," she said, "there's a rabbit."

"It's Snake," said Natalie. "He's got lots of legs and rabbits only have two."

She knew that because her friend Katie had a pink rabbit with two legs and two arms, like other people.

"In the garden," said the lady, "eating the weeds."

"It's all we've got so far," said Mum. "This garden was a field before they built these houses."

Natalie looked outside for something pink, wearing an apron. She saw an animal with a smart brown coat walking by the fence and knew that was a rabbit too.

Mum opened the glass door to let the lady out. The brown rabbit stamped his foot and watched. Natalie watched back. She hoped the rabbit would not shout.

The lady stepped over Natalie and went. The rabbit splashed away through the rain. He had a white tail.

The lady did something quite like that, except for the white tail.

"I must fly," she said. She waved the black

stick, put on some black wings, and flew to the road, and along it.

Natalie hadn't seen people flying before.

"She flew away," she said, watching carefully.

"That's right," said Mum. "She said she would."

"It wasn't a talking stick," said Natalie.

"No," said Mum. "It was an umbrella. Don't go out, Natalie. It's much too wet."

"It was wings," said Natalie. She had seen them.

Mum went back to work in the front room, spreading paste thick on wallpaper and sticking the paper on the pink plaster walls and turning them green and pretty.

"Wings," said Natalie again, just to make sure. "You're safe with me."

"Don't go near the red pail," said Mum. "People can get paste all over themselves, and then get stuck to the wall and make the wallpaper lumpy."

Natalie went to watch for the rabbit. Dolls and toys have to be shown how to be alive on their own.

The rain stopped. Before long the wheelbarrow had no splash-marks on it, and its chin stopped dribbling.

The sun came out, bang, all over the garden, and very soon all the flowers began to show again, yellow, yellow, yellow, and silvery seed-heads.

The rabbit came back, eating dandelions. He scratched his ear. Toys can't do that by themselves.

Mum finished a wall and a corner. "I'll put on one more strip, and it's dinner time," she said. "You can go out and play on the patio for a bit, if you like."

"Quietly," said Natalie. "Don't fly."

"Boots first," said Mum. "Don't take any toys out, because it's still wet."

Natalie did not want to take toys out. She wanted the toy already out there, if it didn't run away wagging its tail. "I'm very kind," she said to Mum.

"I'm sure you are," said Mum.

Natalie went out gently. The rabbit looked at her carefully, and went on eating.

"Rabbit," said Natalie. "You belong to Cecily."

The rabbit did not know about Cecily.

After all, you can't tell from looking at a person like Natalie that she has a baby sister called Cecily. Even Mum didn't know. But Cecily had to have toys of her own, and could start with the rabbit.

Natalie kept quite still. She knew the rabbit would come to her because he looked so nice.

I might keep him, Natalie thought. Cecily can have all the others except Snake with all his legs.

Somebody started shouting. Natalie thought it was the rabbit for a moment, and wondered what she had done. "You are for Cecily, really," she said, very quietly, in case she had thought the wrong thing.

The rabbit jumped into the air, turned round, and ran away through the fence and out of sight.

Somebody went on shouting. There was a

lot of shouting, very cross indeed.

Natalie thought it might be the men building next door, but she could hear them hammering away inside, and the whistling boy happily whistling a lot.

The shouting was in the sky.

Mum heard it and looked out through the window to give Natalie a smile. She was not alarmed, but Natalie did not know what to think, except that she would be safe inside the house.

The noise fell into the garden, and went on happening. Then Natalie knew what it all was, and she still did not like it.

The lady who had flown away with black wings had met another lady with black wings, and they were wrestling in the muddy garden. Other black ladies, dressed as birds, were standing on the roof of the house next door and shouting.

Natalie went indoors at once to complain. Mum spoke first. "Too noisy," she said.

"Don't let her come in the house again," said Natalie. "She frightened away the toys." Because the rabbit belonging to Cecily had run away. "I think I might keep it," she said.

"What are you talking about?" said Mum. "No one wants a load of noisy jackdaws fighting about nests."

"Ladies," said Natalie. "They put up their umbrellas and flew into the garden. Their black talking sticks."

"Birds," said Mum. "I'll send them away."

She went outside and clapped her hands. All the black birds or fighting ladies flew away. Mum went into the middle of the garden and picked things up. She brought them back.

"Put them in the sink," said Natalie.

Mum dropped three black feathers there, and gave Natalie a fluffy white dandelion seed-head. Natalie filled her tummy full of deep breath, and puffed it all out on the seed-head.

"Not in the front room," said Mum, too late.

Little seeds flew everywhere in three puffs, so that was the time.

"Seventeen," said Natalie, the biggest number ever. It used to be three, but it had grown.

Mum picked seeds from the wallpaper

paste, and put the wallpaper up. "Dinner time," she said. "We won't talk about lumps in the wallpaper."

There weren't any, Natalie thought.

Now that the flying ladies, or jackdaws, or umbrellas, had gone, two other visitors were eating the flowers. It was dinner time in the garden too.

"One each," said Natalie. "One rabbit for Cecily. One rabbit for me."

"Cecily?" said Mum.

"I'll tell you one day," said Natalie.

The fence would have to go through some little trees in a place where Natalie played.

STONE

Mum ended the day looking at Natalie in a way that meant she wasn't cross with her but it wasn't to happen again. All she said was, "We'll need them again, one day."

"Yes," said Natalie. "We did."

They had.

The day began with big noises outside making the windows rattle and the floor shake. One doll, who was standing up in a corner, sat down instead. She couldn't bend in the middle so she was lying down, but Natalie knew she meant to sit. Snake with a lot of legs sat on Natalie's pillow and held tight.

Bump, went the noise. Downstairs a door opened and Daddy went out to see what was happening. *Thud, thud, thud* was happening. Natalie saw it from her window. She could feel it in the window sill with her tummy.

Daddy should have come up here to see it, she thought. He could sit beside me and feel it too.

It was the men building that house next door. They once put the floor outside on tall stalks and had races with a wheelbarrow. Now they were putting more stalks into the ground with a machine.

The whistling boy gave the machine wood to hold, and it hit the wood on the head, *bang, bang, bang*, and pushed it into the ground. When a man took the machine away, the wood stood up by itself, and didn't fall over or sit down.

Natalie thought she would like to be the

machine. She could tell what it felt like to be wood.

Mum came to tell her to stop jumping off the bed. "There's enough noise without that," she said.

"Oh," said Natalie. "But I'm doing it quietly."

"It's time to get dressed," said Mum, "and look, Snake doesn't like it. He's fallen on the floor."

Natalie looked on the floor, and got her head in the sleeve of a jumper, and Mum couldn't find her. Daddy did, though, when he came to say goodbye before driving off for the day. He looked up the sleeve and saw Natalie laughing inside.

"It would have been very awkward eating breakfast," said Mum, "getting a spoon up your sleeve."

The yellow wheelbarrow was outside. It

had earth and stones in it, from when it had been helping Daddy put the lawn in the new garden.

Natalie knew what she would do. She told Mum. "I shall wheelbarrow upstairs," she said.

"Actually, no," said Mum.

Thump, thump, thump, went the men and the machine outside.

Whistle, whistle, whistle, went the boy.

Crunch, crunch, crunch, went the breakfast cereal.

"They're putting stalks in," Natalie said, "to make an upstairs outside floor."

"You use that for the wheelbarrow," said Mum. "I shan't mind at all."

Natalie finished breakfast and went to see the floor being made. The men were still putting the posts in, but the floor must be next.

"Do it today," said Natalie to the whistling boy.

"It won't take long," said the boy, giving the machine another piece of wood. "You go back to your mum while we do the noisy bit, eh?"

Natalie went back to Mum. Mum was hanging out washing, and Natalie brought the next lot out to her in the yellow wheelbarrow, taking all the earth and stones out of it first.

"Next time," said Mum, holding up a dirty pillowslip, "we'll wash the barrow as well. But thank you, Natalie, all the same."

Mum carried the rest of the wet washing herself, and some went back to the washing machine. Natalie could see that she had made a mistake, and brought out some more clothes from a cupboard on the landing.

She wanted to take the wheelbarrow up to put them in, but Mum thought it would be better not to take it into the house at all. She always thought that.

"I know you, miss," she said.

"Of course," said Natalie. "I live here."

She got some of her own old clothes from the cupboard – a pink dress, a pink bonnet, and some white tights that were even small for her arm. She brought them down and put them in the wheelbarrow.

Mum had finished with the washing and was talking to the men still making noises with wood.

"I've been waiting for it," she was telling them.

Natalie nodded her head. So had she. She was still waiting for the floor. But when she explained about it the men smiled, and the whistling boy laughed, and Mum said, "It's not a floor, it's the garden fence between us and next door. It will make our garden better."

They must be wrong, Natalie thought. She knew what it would be like on the new floor. She knew she could run about on it all day.

"No floor," said the whistling boy.

But Natalie could see another problem coming. The fence would have to go through some little trees in a place where Natalie played. Daddy had said they were weeds, not trees, told her the name of them, and said she could play in them.

She had a den there, but could not always find it. Once a frog was there and she had to go indoors because it jumped about at her.

Well, she thought, the men can work all that out.

Mum went indoors. Natalie tried to touch

the washing-line but it was up in the sky and out of reach. There was nowhere to hang up a pink dress and bonnet and some white tights.

In the corner of the garden the men were not going round the plants like trees. They were walking through them and squashing them flat.

Natalie went to warn them about the danger of frogs, but they said that the frogs had left early that morning. "I can smell them," said Natalie.

"No," said the whistling boy, "that's the weed you can smell. It's called kelk, and my mum cooks it with rhubarb." He gave her a little piece to smell.

It wasn't the name Daddy had told her.

Another piece of wood went in among the trees called kelk, and one more, and the men stopped, so Natalie had to do something else.

A long shiny black stone lay in the grass, smooth and quiet and sleepy. Natalie had seen it before and wondered what it was, and now she knew it had been put here for her to find, and it was what she wanted.

"You are not a doll," she told it. "You are not me when I was little. You are going to be my new sister and my very own, not Mum's."

Natalie spread the dress over it. She put the tights on it and made the legs straight. She put the bonnet on its head. The stone would have smiled if it had a mouth. It lay there quite happy.

"Baby," she said. She couldn't remember its name, though she knew a baby sister would have one.

She tried to lift it up and put it in the barrow. But it was a heavy baby and would not come up.

Mum decided to go to the shops, and the baby had to be left, with the clothes carefully on it. "Don't do anything naughty," Natalie told it.

After shopping it was dinner, so Natalie forgot to show Mum the new baby until bedtime.

"Well," said Mum, and picked up the dress and bonnet and tights. This was when she looked at Natalie and wasn't cross, and Natalie knew she should not have dressed the stone with those clothes.

Daddy said, "They've put the fence right through that Sweet Cicely in the corner.

I can smell it."

They even know its name, Natalie thought. It was me that forgot it. She said it to the black stone so it would not forget. "Cecily, Cecily, Cecily," and it remembered.

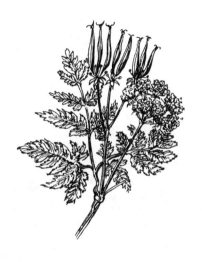

The hedgehog had walked to the plate with the sandwich on. It pulled the sandwich off the plate.

GARDENING

Mum said, "I'll draw the curtains right across, then no one will keep you awake."

Natalie yawned. Her eyes closed all by themselves when she wanted them to stay open. She wanted more than that, but Mum was tucking her in, down the sides and round her neck and kissing her good night.

"I can't cuddle you," said Natalie.

"Your cuddle will sleep with you all night," said Mum.

"I wanted to help Daddy in the garden all day," said Natalie.

"You did," said Mum. "You and your wheelbarrow."

Natalie meant to say a lot more about all day meaning until dark, not just until bedtime, but her eyes stayed closed and it was dark, and…

When her eyes opened it was morning. She heard Daddy outside, and she knew he had been gardening all night. She went down to help him all day.

"Hello, gardener," said Daddy. "Stay on the path."

The path had string along the side of it. Natalie trod on the string with one foot, tripped over it with the other, hit her toes on a stone and pricked her heels with a thistle.

Daddy was going to pick her up before she got miserable and her nightie wet and muddy.

"Don't," she said. "I'm talking." There was a black shiny thing crawling over a leaf and waving at her with telescope eyes. Natalie waved hers back, though they were not on stalks.

"A black slug," said Daddy. "We'll never have a garden because slugs eat everything that grows."

He had forgotten about all the dandelions. And there was the kelk, or Sweet Cecily, like trees in the corner, where Natalie had her den and could get lost if she tried.

The slug waved goodbye, and Natalie went in to have her own breakfast, and to wave goodbye to Daddy.

She finished with a long drink of very quick milk, and while Mum was drying her ears after it, Natalie saw someone else in the garden.

"Stay on the path," she told it. But it took no notice of her. It pushed its way under the string, and walked about on the place that was going to be lawn. It was looking for something.

"Hedgehog," said Mum. "I wonder what she lost. Shoes on first, Natalie."

Natalie was going out at once to help the hedgehog. By the time her shoes were on, the hedgehog had found what it was looking for.

"It's playing with my black slug," said Natalie. "They're playing tickling." The hedgehog was rolling the slug about with its front paws. The slug had folded its eyes down and showed its white tummy, and wasn't laughing very loud. It might really want to play something gentler, like waving its eyes.

We're friends, thought Natalie. You can come to my party. "Just me and Cecily," she told them. "My sister. All of us could play."

But only the hedgehog was listening. It

had been having a party of its own, and eaten the slug. It made a lot of noise about it, and went on swallowing after it had finished.

"Then I'll just play with you," said Natalie. "You have to stay on the path for this game."

It took a long time for the game to start, because first Natalie had to get the yellow wheelbarrow for the hedgehog to ride in.

"What are you doing?" Mum called from the kitchen.

"Just a problem," said Natalie. The hedgehog had folded itself up like a prickly sack, no nose, no paws, no eyes, no tail. "All its bones are sticking out and I can't pick it up. And it's eaten my slug."

She tipped the barrow on its side, rolled the hedgehog into it with a saucer, then lifted the barrow upright, and there was the hedgehog, having a ride up the garden path.

"Sploosh," said Natalie, at the end of the path, tipping the hedgehog out. She hoped the workmen would appear and see how good she was at the job.

She got the hedgehog into the barrow again and brought it back to the house.

"Sploosh, Mum," she called, and unloaded the hedgehog again. The hedgehog slid on to the path and stayed quite still.

Mum came out and took Natalie's hand. She held it very kindly and softly. She did not say anything.

"But I like rides," Natalie was beginning to say. But she was thinking that hedgehogs might not like rides in a yellow wheelbarrow or being *splooshed* out.

And she thought that Mum had explained that by holding her hand so gently and not saying anything. So that Natalie had said it all to herself, and explained to herself how unkind she had been.

She was very sorry. Her eyes went as prickly as a hedgehog, and she was crying for it.

"There," said Mum. "We don't always know before we do things, do we?"

"I was just showing it the path," said Natalie, very lumpily, just as if she had been in the yellow wheelbarrow and bouncing up and down.

"Your nose is running everywhere," said Mum. "We'll go in and see to that, then you can come out and talk to the hedgehog again. You didn't mean to, but you must have frightened it."

Natalie had her face washed. As well as all the runniness there was still breakfast milk in her ears.

She took her dinner out with her. It was a little sandwich with ham in it, the soft sort from a tin.

She put the plate on the ground and got into the barrow. It was quite comfortable, if you were Natalie. She tried being her baby sister, but the baby sister wasn't in the mood for that.

Mum came to the door again. "Have you said sorry?" she asked. "Can you do it before your dinner."

Natalie got up from the barrow. The hedgehog was still curled up where it had been *splooshed*.

"Sorry," said Natalie. "Don't be frightened."

The hedgehog said nothing. It did not move.

"Sorry, sorry," said Natalie.

She got into the barrow again. She thought she heard a noise of hedgehog uncurling, being unfrightened. She sat up too suddenly, and *splooshed* herself out sideways when the wheelbarrow fell over.

The hedgehog was still curled up like a cottage loaf.

It wants new batteries, Natalie thought. "Wake up," she said, but still nothing happened.

"I can't have my dinner till you do," said Natalie. "I shan't feel hungry till then."

She waited. She watched. She began to get cross with a hedgehog who wouldn't wake up, but she knew that was wrong. If she was cross she would not be sorry, and she had to mean it when she said it.

The hedgehog twitched. One end shuffled along a bit. Natalie expected its nose to appear. But it was the back end that had wriggled. Then the other end uncurled, and there was the nose. The eyes were there too. They looked round. The nose twitched. The hedgehog walked.

"I'm sorry," said Natalie. "I was only giving you a ride. Hedgehog, what are you doing?"

The hedgehog had walked to the plate with the sandwich on. It pulled the sandwich off the plate.

It had rolled the slug about, then eaten it.

Now it rolled the sandwich about, and then it ate it. It swallowed it for a long time, and then it walked away.

Natalie watched it go. She picked up the plate with nothing on it. She took it into the kitchen.

"There now," said Mum. "Did you enjoy that?"

"It was the best meal I ever had," said Natalie, now that the hedgehog had forgiven her.

*Somebody began walking beside her,
on the other side of the fence.*

Buying and Selling

Natalie was reading a book of animals when Mum went outside to talk to somebody. Natalie thought of going to help, but the book was too comfortable to be put down. She was on her back, with her hands on two top corners of the pages, and her feet in the air holding up the other two corners.

I'd better stay like this for ever, she thought. It won't ever come right again.

She would have got up if Mum was talking to the whistling boy from the builders next door. But no one was whistling, so that it couldn't be him.

In the end the book fell down on her and

all the pictures went back inside. Natalie had nothing to hold her feet up and that didn't feel right. But she knew that if she ever met a lion or a little deer she would stroke it, or pet the naughty square brown dog.

"Never mind," said Mum. She had stopped talking outside. "Stop grumbling, put your shoes on, and we'll go shopping."

When they went out, furniture was being carried into the house next door. There was a van full of it in the road. There was a huge sofa and two tall lamps.

"But what's it for?" asked Natalie.

"People are going to live there," said Mum.

"My whistling boy?" said Natalie.

"Some people we don't know yet," said Mum. "We came to our new house and they are coming to theirs."

Natalie had read the book, so she knew the

people. They would be round and blue and wooden, and have the square brown dog. "I know," she said. "It is a very bad dog."

At the shop Natalie pushed the trolley. The yellow wheelbarrow would have been better, and more comfortable too if you needed a ride. She went to the shelves and got some of the things they needed. Mum put a lot of them back.

Mum walked past the boxes with babies on the outside. Natalie wanted to buy one and find a sister inside, with its nappy on.

They had a drink and a cheese roll at the café. The cress got into Natalie's nose.

There was a baby at another table. The café people brought it a bottle to drink.

It wouldn't be any trouble, thought Natalie. I wasn't. She could have the pink dress. I know where it is.

*   *   *

When they got home the big sofa and the lamps, and the whole van, had gone away.

Natalie went into the garden to find things. "I shall fill the wheelbarrow right up," she said. She really wanted to bring in the stone called Cecily that she had once dressed to be her sister. She would not *sploosh* it out of the wheelbarrow, but would teach it to walk, and how to dress itself.

But you need the wheelbarrow to put it in first of all, and the barrow was not to be seen. It ought to be standing in the garden, on the new path, or on the lawn at the front, or on the gravel.

Natalie was walking past the new fence when something happened that explained what was wrong.

Somebody began walking beside her, on the other side of the fence. The fence had a piece of wood standing up, and then a piece that wasn't there, and then one that was, and one that wasn't, nearly all the way along, because it wasn't quite finished.

Somebody walked beside her. When she put her foot down, that other person put its foot down. When she put the other foot down and moved on, so did that other person.

When she stopped, so did that other person.

When she turned and looked through the fence, so did that other person.

There was a mouth, and a nose, and two eyes looking into hers. And that was the shape Natalie was, she knew. There were hands, and Natalie had hands too.

She turned away and walked on a bit further. The other person walked too. They stopped together.

Natalie ran along the fence. The other

person ran as well.

Natalie stretched her arms out. The other person stretched arms out.

Just like me, Natalie thought. But how could anyone be like her?

In the grass behind that other person was the yellow wheelbarrow.

Then I did find it, said Natalie to herself. But I didn't as well, because I'm not me any longer. That person over there is me, so who am I?

I am not my little sister Cecily, she decided. I am too big for the pink dress and white tights.

And she wanted the yellow wheelbarrow, and it was hers, and she was Natalie, and another person was not allowed to be Natalie.

"Stop being me," she said.

"I'm not you," said the other person. "I

never was. I am Alistair. I just live here."

"Give me back my wheelbarrow," said Natalie. "I've lived here for a long time, so it's mine, not yours."

"I'm using it," said Alistair.

Natalie could deal with that, now that she was sure who she was. She walked along the fence to where the kelk, or Sweet Cecily, grew, and the fence was not quite finished and had big gaps in it.

Alistair walked along with her, the other side.

Natalie went through a gap. Now she was the same side as Alistair, and could not get muddled.

"I like your barrow best," said Alistair.

"I need it," said Natalie. "It's from my garden."

"I would like to keep it," said Alistair.

"So would I," said Natalie. "You can see it

my side if you look through the fence."

"I don't need to," said Alistair. "It's my side already." He stroked the wheelbarrow. "I like it most," he said. "I really do."

All Natalie had to do was wheel it away. But Alistair wanted to think it was his too.

"I will buy it," he said.

"It isn't in a shop," said Natalie. "Silly boy."

"I will give you something instead," said Alistair.

"You haven't got anything," said Natalie.

Alistair's best things were still packed in boxes because they had been in the van with the furniture, but he found something that Natalie would really like.

"Its eyes aren't open yet," he explained. Natalie took it, and gave him the barrow to wheel up and down his wild garden.

Natalie wheeled her thing from Alistair's

patio through the gap in the fence, and took it to show Mum.

"Goodness," said Mum. "Where did you get that?"

"I bought it," said Natalie. "From Alistair."

"We must take it back," said Mum. "At once."

"Alistair doesn't like it," said Natalie. "And we've got clothes for it, and the push chair."

"I'm sure it's very nice really," said Mum. "But it is someone else's baby and not ours at all."

Natalie knew that this was really Alistair's baby sister, not her own. "It was nice having her," she said, "but her eyes aren't open yet."

And she was missing the wheelbarrow already.

The mum next door hadn't missed her baby, but she was glad to have her back. Alistair offered to share the yellow wheelbarrow with Natalie.

"What was the baby called?" Mum asked later.

Natalie could not say Cecily. But she knew the name the whistling boy had taught her.

"Kelk," she said. "Just Kelk."

*Alistair was beside her, holding her arm and helping
her up, sitting her down, looking at her eyes.*

DANDELION CLOCKS

Alistair had something that must really belong to her, Natalie thought.

But Alistair said, "Mine," and took it from Natalie when she picked it up.

"It belongs to my whistling boy," said Natalie.

If it belonged to her whistling boy, then it belonged to Natalie. She would know the whistling boy's building trowel anywhere, with its sort of flat spoon to mix *sploosh* with, a clever bend so that the *sploosh* didn't get up your sleeve, and then a wooden handle.

"It was in my garden," said Alistair. It was still in his garden. He and Natalie were there.

"You stole my yellow wheelbarrow from my garden," said Natalie. "So you stole this."

She had been sitting down, but now she stood up. Alistair sat on the grass and held the trowel close to him. "Only mine," he said.

"It's a doll," said Natalie. She knew that boys were not good at liking dolls when anyone was there.

Alistair hugged the trowel tighter. "Yes," he said. He turned it so that the clever bend held the wooden handle tight against his neck. He didn't care.

Natalie turned round and walked away. She was going to take the yellow wheelbarrow away for ever. She looked round for it, somewhere in Alistair's big garden. It was so near that she did not see it and fell over it. Her head dropped down on the ground, and there was a puff of smoke. Dandelion clocks floated up as if there was a fire.

I am going to cry, Natalie thought. I can.

Then Alistair was beside her, holding her arm and helping her up, sitting her down, looking at her eyes.

I can't, thought Natalie. He's looking.

Alistair was more than looking. He was putting something into her arms for her to hold.

It was the whistling boy's trowel, and its handle could hold itself against her neck.

I've got to, thought Natalie. But I won't cry because he took the whistling boy's spoon, and I won't cry because he gave it back, and I won't cry because I fell over my wheelbarrow. So I can't.

Alistair picked up the wheelbarrow. Perhaps it will cry, thought Natalie. But it stood there on its wheel and its elbows, and it didn't cry.

Natalie thought of giving back the trowel. She started to, but that was too hard. Instead she laid it in the barrow. Of course that was where trowels often lived, stuck in the *sploosh*. This one was lost, though, so it had to do without *sploosh*.

"Give it a ride," she told Alistair. She had decided it was a boy's toy, a boy's doll, and that Alistair could look after it.

Alistair picked up the barrow handles. "We'll go shopping," he said.

Shopping was not very far. Alistair bumped the barrow up the garden until he reached Natalie's den in the tall trees. The wheelbarrow turned into a shopping trolley, and they took it into the sweet-smelling shop, under the pretty green leaves.

I'm not crying, Natalie thought. That's

sad. I really need to. She bought things from the shelves. No one told her to put them back. She could have as much as she liked.

Nothing fell out of the trolley. The trowel baby did not shriek or howl. Alistair piled the trolley higher and higher. Then they couldn't take it any further into the shop, because there was a thin wiry fence hidden amongst the leaves, and made of rust.

They went back to the checkout, and Alistair got a lot of cash-back. Natalie filled the bags.

She knew what else to do. An egg roll in the café was next, under the leaves. Alistair had a toffee biscuit. Natalie cut up her egg roll with the trowel.

Not far away someone was whistling. They were not the only ones having dinner. A black bird came down into Alistair's garden with a bun of its own, and started to eat it. It looked all round between pecks, and it swallowed big lumps. The black bird had a real bun, but Natalie had a play egg roll.

Another black bird came down to help eat the bun.

"They will fight," said Natalie. She had seen black birds before. "One is an umbrella lady."

The two birds started arguing. One pecked the other. One of them fell over and the other jumped on him. They both looked very cross.

"Do you know them?" asked Alistair.

"No," said Natalie. "I'm just frightened." She thought she might get frightened enough to cry, so no one would know it was really about Alistair thinking the trowel was his.

One bird flew up into the air with most of the bun, and the other began to follow. The bird with the bun began by flying straight. Then it flew sideways, gave a big shout, and dropped the bun.

The bun fell straight down and landed just beside Natalie. It had muddy clawmarks on it, and all the best bits had gone.

Somebody else shouted. A stone flew among the leaves of the café and dropped to the ground.

Natalie and Alistair ran straight out, into the garden again. Natalie thought it was very naughty of the black birds to drop stones on people in shops.

It had not been a bird dropping stones. At the other side of the wire fence was Natalie's whistling boy.

"Eh well," he said, shaking his head. "Did I throw a stone at you? I thought it was two birds."

"The birds flew away," said Natalie.

"They had a fight first," said Alistair.

"I was frightened," said Natalie.

"I didn't mean to frighten you," said the whistling boy. "One of those birds took my bun out of my bag."

"It's here," said Natalie. She looked at the bun and did not want to touch it. Nor did the boy.

Alistair put the stone in the trolley beside the trowel and wheeled the barrow out of the café.

"Well, I maybe lost my dinner," said the whistling boy. "But you've found my trowel."

"It's mine," said Alistair. "I found it first."

Natalie picked it up, took it to the fence, and gave it to the whistling boy. "You can have your dinner in our café," she said. "Do you want soup?"

"I'll be off home for a minute," said the

whistling boy. "It's just close by." And off he went.

He's always right, thought Natalie. You can't eat soup with a flat spoon.

"He can have it back," said Alistair. "Because he didn't get any dinner."

"He's my whistling boy," said Natalie. "And this is my wheelbarrow."

"And this is my house," said Alistair.

"And they were your horrible birds," said Natalie. "And I am going home because you have made me cry."

She still needed to cry. It was all ready inside her head. She had such a struggle getting the wheelbarrow through a gap in the fence that she lost the stone the whistling boy had thrown. She found several that might be the right one, but left them to play on their own, and forgot to cry.

"I was just coming for you," said Mum.

"It's dinner time."

"It's that sort of day," said Natalie. "There were umbrellas fighting, and the whistling boy threw a stone at them and I lost it, and he got his *sploosh* spoon back. I can't stand it. I'm going to cry."

"Wash your hands first," said Mum, "and then your face won't get all streaky."

There was such a nice sausage for dinner that the crying went away.

Some days nothing comes right.

*There were one, two, three,
four candles on the cake.*

CANDLES

Natalie ran through to Mum, who was in the kitchen waving a red party jelly. She had something important to say.

"Careful," said Mum. "If this drops on the floor it won't come back together again."

Natalie thought it would be fun if the jelly wobbled about on the floor. It could still be eaten. But Mum thought it would unjelly, and be no use.

"Go back to the table and look after all your friends," Mum went on to say. "It's your birthday party, so you enjoy it. We'll do all the work." She meant herself and the mums of the party guests.

Natalie got halfway to the table, then remembered what she had been going to say, and went to tell Mum again. It was important.

"It's Alistair," said Natalie. "He's too little."

"He's about the same as you," said Mum. "He had his birthday before he came to live next door. I expect you'll go to his party next year."

"He can't count properly," said Natalie. She explained how Alistair had seen the birthday cake and straight away had said, "Four candles."

"Right," said Mum. "That's where you've got to."

"I know," said Natalie. "But you don't just say 'four' like that. If you can really count you say, 'One, two, three, four'. You always do."

Mum gave the jelly to another mum to hold, because it was wobbling dangerously.

"I meant to tell you this morning," said Mum. "But we were so busy, weren't we? Now you're four you just say the biggest number and not all the little ones. Alistair is four already, so that's what he does."

That seemed sensible to Natalie. It seemed more than sensible, because now she could suit herself.

"The biggest number is seven," she said. "That's what I'll be, seven, seven, seven."

But there were one, two, three, four candles on the cake. Next year, thought Natalie, seven.

Before cutting the cake there was lighting the candles with a very long match. Natalie held the match, with Mum nearly helping her, but the candles were not keeping still.

Daddy came home just then and held

Natalie's hand steady, so that all four candles stood straight up and had burning hair, and looked so happy. Natalie sucked a hot finger that tasted of matches.

"Happy fourth birthday," said Alistair. He had had his fourth birthday so he knew what to say.

Natalie took a deep breath. "One," she said, and blew out a candle. It was like puffing dandelion clocks into the air. "Two," and blew another, and "Three," and the last one. "Seven," she said. "Seven o'clock. I'm oldest."

She began to cut the cake, with a silver trowel like the one belonging to the whistling boy. He should have come to the party and used his real trowel, but you can't have everyone, Mum said.

"I'll get the ice-cream," said Mum when the cake had been cut up a bit and most people did not eat it.

The party went on but Alistair, or Katie, won the games.

In real life, the birthday girl wins all the games. "It's what you have a birthday for," Natalie told Mum, in case she hadn't noticed.

"Not really," said Mum. "You let the guests win."

"I'll tell them to lose," said Natalie.

"These aren't winning and losing games," said Mum. "They're joining-in games, and you all get a sweet."

Alistair burst a balloon and cried.

By then Natalie wanted to go to bed before the party was over, so she could wear one of her presents.

"My new nightie," she said, getting it out of the golden bag. "With a shark on the front."

"It's a dragon," said Alistair. It was.

"It keeps changing," said Natalie. She did not want Alistair to be right all the time. She wanted to put the nightie on and be whatever it was.

The guests went home. They got presents too, but they weren't Natalie's presents, so that was fair.

When Natalie came downstairs again after her bath, wearing the dragon nightie, the party had been tidied away. Her other presents were on a little table, and Daddy was taking away all the wrapping paper and bags.

"I need those," said Natalie. "I am going to wrap everything up again, so I need some sticky tape too. I'll just wear the nightie."

"We thought you liked presents," said Mum. "Aren't you going to keep them?"

"No way," said Natalie. "Tomorrow I am

going to get up and have my party all over again but I am going to start at the end and have jelly first, and no one is coming, and I am going to win all the games."

Also, she pointed out, the balloons have not got to burst. Alistair has not got to burst any balloons. They are not to make that noise and hurt you down your inside. Me down my inside.

"You'll end up three years old again," said Daddy.

Natalie had to explain about not counting one, two, three, four any more. "If there is only four, you can't count backwards," she said.

In the morning she got up – at night, she said. She had not slept in the dragon nightie, because she was taking it off and they hadn't had that night. It was very simple if you knew how.

On the table downstairs were all her presents, wrapped up again. Natalie folded the nightie and put it back in its bag, and gave it to herself.

"Breakfast?" said Mum. "Before the party? If you are living backwards."

"Jelly and ice-cream," said Natalie. "Then running about with music and not moving when it stops."

Natalie was good at that game when other people weren't winning instead. She won four times.

The cake was not complete, but no one likes birthday cake so that doesn't matter, and all the candles were easier to light today.

"You should blow them out first," said Mum.

"It's my birthday," said Natalie. "I am going to do it my own way."

Natalie blew out the candles one by one,

with no one bothering her or helping her.

"This is the best way to have a party," she said.

She had sandwiches and orange drink. No one burst a balloon. Nobody counted wrong. No one else won any of the games. Natalie passed the parcel to herself, and after only the third time the music stopped and she got the sweet in the middle.

Then all the guests went home, because that was where they were before they got here.

"I don't understand it all," said Mum.

"They've gone," said Natalie. "I need my present too." The present was a hanky with nursery rhymes on it. And there were the other presents too, on the small table. Natalie opened them one by one, and she was pleased all over again. She watched the Magic Islands video for a bit, then undid the last present, the nightie.

She had expected to find it all new again, but it was wrinkled.

"Someone has been sleeping in it," she said, because she was still at the party and hadn't gone to bed, she knew.

"Oh," said Mum, "that's what they do these days, to get them warm for the birthday person."

"Oh, I forgot," said Natalie. "You see, going to bed hasn't happened yet."

"Well, happy birthday," said Mum.

"It was all right," said Natalie. "Both times were better."

Natalie showed Alistair how she would arrange the
house for the summer, which is what it was for.

The House in Summer

Natalie saw her whistling boy in the front garden one morning.

"My whistling boy," she said.

"He can't whistle," said Mum. She was not looking out of the window, and thought Natalie meant Alistair. "Can you whistle, Natalie?"

Natalie knew about whistling. Your mouth went like this. Or it went like that. And you could smile at the same time. *Whistle, whistle*, you could go.

"Not with breakfast cereal in your mouth," said Daddy, getting a tissue and mopping up some whistled milk. Then he left his cup of tea and went out to talk to the whistling boy, and lift some house-building stuff from a truck.

"I usually can," said Natalie. She could often hear herself whistling.

"It's all in your mind," said Mum. "And I'm sure it's all in Alistair's mind too. He can't quite whistle yet."

"Of course not," said Natalie. But she had not been thinking of Alistair. She decided that Cecily could probably whistle, if everyone thought hard about it. Her sister would be born whistling, except for not being born at all.

The whistling boy solved the problem by having a very loud whistle, the one that Natalie knew best. Mum heard it indoors, and saw him from the window.

"We're both right," she said. "Alistair can't whistle, and that big boy can."

"My whistling boy," said Natalie. "I don't go about with children."

Natalie went out to see about the building stuff. She thought the house was finished, but they didn't tell her everything. She mentioned this to Mum.

"You didn't say you wanted to know," said Mum. "Tell us what you want us to tell you."

"I think I'll go outside," said Natalie. Whistling boys were much more sensible, she knew.

Daddy was carrying a kind of wall, made of wood nailed together. It had wavy edges all across it, like knitting.

The whistling boy said, "Mind yourself, missis," and went past Natalie carrying a huge piece of the same knitted wall.

There were more pieces, big ones and little ones, and they were all put against the fence. The whistling boy brought a door.

There was a big piece of paper with drawings and writing on. Daddy went into the house again to finish his breakfast. His cup of tea was cold.

The whistling boy drove the truck away.

After all that, nothing was happening. The whistling boy had only told her to mind herself, missis, and then gone away.

He probably doesn't know he's the whistling boy, thought Natalie. He probably thinks he's just himself. I will ask him one day.

For now she had to make do with Alistair. Alistair was riding up and down his garden on a trike and not taking any notice of Natalie.

"It's because he can't whistle," Natalie told Mum.

"You could go through the fence," said Mum. "His mother wouldn't mind."

"It's my turn to ride his trike," said Natalie. "Because he is having a better time than me."

Before she got to the fence the whistling boy drove back in the truck and stopped outside the house again.

This time he had brought his wheelbarrow. It was upside down with its elbows in the air, and its wheel going round on its own.

Natalie got her yellow wheelbarrow out and waited to help the whistling boy, and wheel with him wherever he wheeled.

He did not wheel. He left the barrow on the truck and instead brought some digging things.

"Pickaxe," said Daddy, coming out to help and carrying the pickaxe.

"Shovel," said the whistling boy, waving one.

"Just digging out a base for a summer-house," said the whistling boy, at the back fence.

Daddy was measuring with a long tape. "About here, I think." He lifted up the pickaxe and hit it into the ground. Then he pulled it out again.

When he had done it several times the whistling boy shovelled soil out and threw it to one side.

Just making a hole, Natalie decided.

She went to see Alistair. She had to go through to him.

"I can't come through today," he said. "Or we'll get in the way."

"Can you whistle?" said Natalie.

They whistled until they were dizzy, but they couldn't get a tune. They were so dizzy that Natalie did not see what was starting in her own garden. She went through the fence to look. Alistair had to stay behind.

The hole was finished. It was very tidy and square, with wood round it. Daddy was pleased, and Natalie was just in time to be very close to what happened next.

The whistling boy had got the wheelbarrow from the truck and put it the right way up. The truck was full of *sploosh*, and the boy had filled the barrow with it, and brought it to the neat square hole.

And *splooshed* it in.

Daddy stood in the hole next to the *sploosh* and stirred it with the shovel, and spread it out. The whistling boy went back for another helping.

Natalie went down with the yellow wheelbarrow and had a side order of *sploosh*, and wheeled it down the garden.

"Just the two of us," said the whistling boy.

Alistair watched from the other side of the fence.

Then all the work was done, and the *sploosh* made quite flat and shiny.

"Finished," said the whistling boy, taking his barrow, and his pickaxe and his shovel and the truck and going away without saying goodbye.

Alistair came through the fence after dinner. "We can't go near," he said.

"No," said Natalie. "They told me that too."

They only went near enough to touch the shiny *sploosh* with their fingers and make marks like paws.

Daddy came out and sent Alistair home for now. Mum rinsed Natalie's fingers and was not pleased with her.

The next day, when Natalie had gone to bed but it was still light outside, the whistling boy came back. Natalie looked past the curtain to see him. His truck was empty, so she did not know why he was here.

In the morning there was a house at the bottom of the garden, with a door and windows and a roof.

The door was not locked. Natalie went in. The *sploosh* had turned hard and now it was the floor. It's mine, Natalie thought. I'll put my bed here.

She heard Alistair calling, and coming to visit.

She closed the door. Alistair tried to come in, but she would not let him. "Knock," she said.

He knocked. But she still would not let him in.

"Ring the bell," she told him.

"There isn't one," said Alistair.

"Then you can't come in," said Natalie.

"Then I won't," said Alistair.

"Oh," said Natalie, because he thought she meant it, and she knew it was only a game. "Men!" She pulled him in. "Really."

It would be best if it was the whistling boy, she thought. He would understand. But she showed Alistair how she would arrange the house for the summer, which is what it was for, and they spent the whole summer in there, all that morning.

Alistair was looking at something…
Natalie saw what he saw. She knew what it was.

THIRD BEDROOM

There were three bedrooms upstairs in Natalie's house. She had counted them, one, two, three, when she was little, and now she was older, just three by itself.

Mum was busy painting the little bedroom. "It might come in useful," she said. "Wallpaper tomorrow. Grandpa might come to stay. Anybody."

"Whistling boy," said Natalie, and Mum laughed. She doesn't know what's important, Natalie decided.

Of course, there might be something even better than the whistling boy.

"You never tell me what's important," said

Natalie. She went outside to see what to do about it. But she would never get it upstairs by herself, even if she found it. It was the right size, but it was heavy.

Daddy had moved the black stone that was called Cecily. Instead of leaving the garden tidy he was making paths and heaps of rubbish. Perhaps he had buried the stone. When it hasn't even been born, Natalie remembered, and I can't find it.

The third bedroom was finished and its smell went away. Mum was taking it easy and Daddy was doing shopping and even cooked all the dinner one day in the garden, having a barbecue for Alistair's mum and dad. Natalie got some black meat to eat, very hard. She put it on one of the rubbish heaps.

She found the black stone Cecily there, face up under the weeds, with tears in her eyes and a slug for a smile. Natalie wiped her dry and rolled her out of the heap. She was still a heavy baby, and wouldn't crawl. And someone was crying.

It was Alistair's sister who was crying. Her mother was tickling her, Mum was wanting to hold her, and Alistair was looking the other way.

Daddy and Alistair's dad ate the last of the cooking, and the mums sat in chairs outside the summerhouse.

Alistair came to help Natalie. The stone baby would keep going in circles. In the end Natalie called Daddy to move the baby for them.

"No problem," he said, picking it up and dropping it back on the heap of rubbish.

"It's a baby," Natalie shouted.

"You don't need it," said Daddy.

But, "It's Cecily, my sister," Natalie said, all sorry and bubbly with tears.

"It's all right, Natalie," said Mum. "We've got three bedrooms and soon we'll have another real baby. If it's a girl what shall we call it?"

"Cecily," said Natalie.

"And if it's a boy," said Daddy, "what then?"

"Whistling," said Natalie, thinking it was a good joke. Everybody thought it was a good joke, and that was lucky, because often they had no sense of humour.

Now Natalie wanted to do some house-keeping herself, to be ready for the baby. She hoped it might be next week, or tomorrow, or after tea, but it seemed to be coming at Christmas.

Probably a present for me, Natalie thought.

She could not get into the summerhouse to housekeep, because it was full of sleepy dads and mums.

Natalie and Alistair went to make a den in the tall smelly stuff called kelk. "Sweet Cecily," Natalie said. "It's like trees. I am as big as a tree."

They began to pull stalks down, pick the green seeds from the tops, and throw them at each other.

They pulled their way right to the back, and there was the rusty back fence of the garden. Alistair went over the bottom wire, and Natalie went under it.

There were real trees here. Natalie was lost at once. She only knew gardens, not this forest.

"Nobody wants us," said Natalie. "They aren't saying our names." She wished they would.

Alistair was standing under a tree. "I can touch the lowest branch," he said. "It's bigger than me."

They found an apple on it. The apple was out of reach. They found a tree with plums. A wasp lived there and scribbled about in the air with loud words.

Natalie thought there was a baby shouting for them. But the baby wasn't due until Christmas.

Alistair ran ahead. It was a downhill place, and Natalie had to fall over twice to keep up with him.

Alistair was looking at something. He had great big round eyes. He could not stop looking, though he wanted to turn and tell Natalie what he had seen. He was so busy looking he could not even speak.

Natalie saw what he saw. She knew what it was. She did not have to stare at it. All she had to do was walk towards it and pat it on the head.

"It's a little deer," she said. "In the woods."

"I thought it was a lion," said Alistair.

"That's on the other page," said Natalie. It was on the other page in her book, she told him.

"It would eat me," said Alistair.

Natalie was trying to stroke the white animal. It kept lifting up its mouth and taking hold of her fingers. "This is eating me," said Natalie.

The animal had a look at Alistair. He had his hands behind him, in case of being eaten too. "It probably is a lion," he said. "It might be a silly book you read." Then he sat down, because the animal bumped him in the tummy.

"Take it away," he told Natalie.

"It's on a lead," said Natalie. "We'll take it home. Your sister can ride on it."

Natalie took hold of the animal's lead, but it was an iron chain that caught her fingers, and the animal was not good like Grandpa's dog. It was bad, like the wind slamming the door. It hurt her fingers.

She was just about to cry, because she didn't want her fingers hurt, or the little white deer to be so naughty. Alistair was nearly crying too.

Someone came and rescued them. "Now," he said, "what's our little goat doing with you?"

Natalie felt safe at once. She was so safe she sat down and cried and it was lovely. Alistair rubbed his nose, and it ran a lot. His eyes went pink and tears dropped out of them.

Nothing could go wrong now, because they had been rescued by the whistling boy. He knew we were here, Natalie thought, and he found us before we were lost.

"Come on, our goat," said the whistling boy. The goat was good at once.

"It's a little white deer," Natalie reminded him.

"It's a lion," said Alistair.

"It's a tiger," said the whistling boy. "If it gets going. Now, let's get you home, out of our orchard."

All four of them went up the hill, and then there was a building Natalie had never seen before. For a moment she thought they were all lost again.

"I built that little summerhouse," said the whistling boy. "With your dad. Is there anybody in?"

Everybody was in. Several of them were asleep, and Alistair's sister was cry-babying to herself.

The whistling boy lifted Alistair over the

fence. He lifted Natalie over. She waited for the little white deer to come next, and then the whistling boy.

But now a baby was coming there would be no third bedroom for the whistling boy, so he went off down the hill, to go home and live there, whistling loudly.

But he's still mine, thought Natalie. When he is lost I will find him and bring him home.

"We'd better wake up," Mum was saying. "Have you had a nice time, Natalie?"

Alistair was looking at his baby sister. "You can have her if you want," he said.

"No," said Natalie. "That's an old one. I'm getting a new one in a box. They're better, and they never cry."

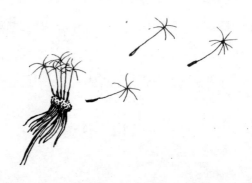